T. Tudor

The Night
Before Christmas

The Night Before Christmas

CLEMENT CLARKE MOORE

ILLUSTRATED BY
TASHA TUDOR

SIMON & SCHUSTER BOOKS FOR YOUNG READERS

SIMON & SCHUSTER BOOKS FOR YOUNG READERS
An imprint of Simon & Schuster Children's Publishing Division
1230 Avenue of the Americas, New York, New York 10020

Typography by Heather Wood
The text for this book is set in Weiss.
The illustrations are rendered in watercolor.
Printed and bound in the United States of America
First Simon & Schuster Books for Young Readers Edition, 1997
1   3   5   7   9   10   8   6   4   2

Library of Congress Cataloging-in-Publication Data
Moore, Clement Clarke, 1779-1863
The night before Christmas / written by Clement Clarke Moore ; illustrated by Tasha Tudor.
p.   cm.
Summary: The illustrator's Vermont farmhouse and her pets are featured in the illustrations
of this well-known poem about an important Christmas Eve visitor.
ISBN 0-689-81375-9
1. Santa Claus—Juvenile poetry. 2. Christmas—Juvenile poetry. 3. Children's poetry, American. [1. Santa Claus—Poetry.
2. Christmas—Poetry. 3. American poetry. 4. Narrative poetry.] I. Tudor, Tasha, ill. II. Title.
PS2429.M5N5   1997b   811'.2—dc21   96-48760

The Night
Before Christmas

'Twas the night before Christmas,
when all through the house

Not a creature was stirring,
not even a mouse.

The stockings were hung
by the chimney with care,

In hopes that Saint Nicholas
soon would be there.

The children were nestled
all snug in their beds,

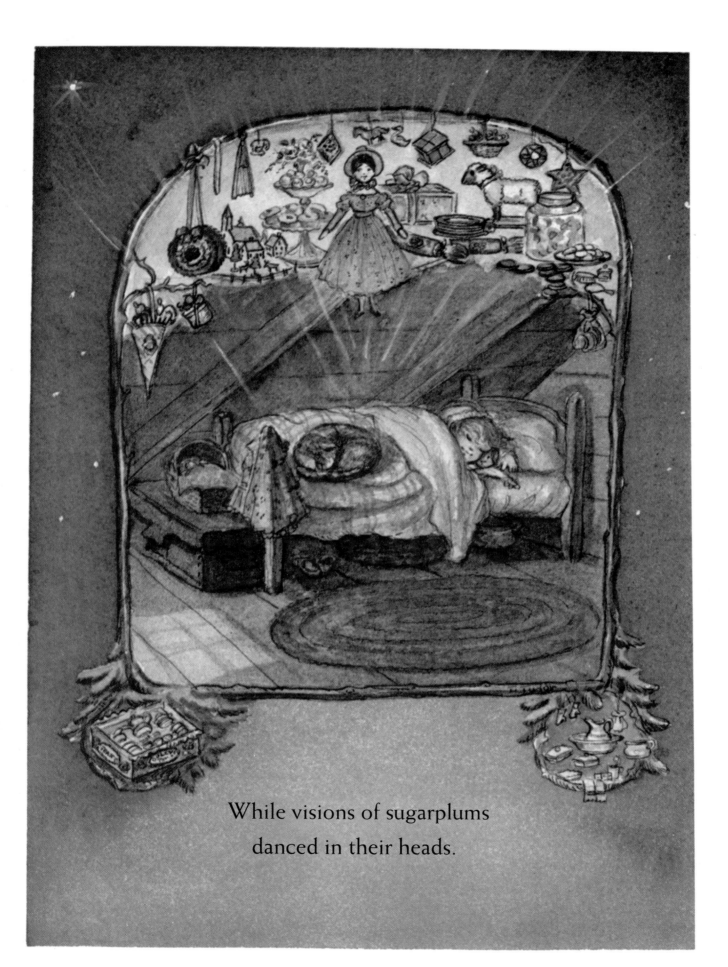

While visions of sugarplums
danced in their heads.

And Mama in her kerchief
and I in my cap

Had just settled our brains
for a long winter's nap,

When out on the lawn
there arose such a clatter,

I sprang from my bed
to see what was the matter.

Away to the window
I flew like a flash,

Tore open the shutters
and threw up the sash.

The moon on the breast
of the new-fallen snow
Gave the luster of midday
to objects below,

When what to my wondering
eyes should appear,
But a miniature sled
and eight tiny reindeer,

With a little old driver
so lively and quick,

I knew in a moment
it must be St. Nick.

More rapid than eagles
his coursers they came,
And he whistled and shouted
and called them by name:

"Now, Dasher! Now, Dancer!
Now, Prancer and Vixen!
On Comet! On Cupid!
On Donder and Blitzen!

To the top of the porch,
to the top of the wall!

Now dash away! Dash away!
Dash away all!"

As dry leaves that before
the wild hurricane fly
When they meet with an obstacle,
mount to the sky,

So up to the housetop
the coursers they flew,
With the sleigh full of toys
and St. Nicholas too.

And then, in a twinkling,
I heard on the roof
The prancing and pawing
of each little hoof.

As I drew in my head
    and was turning around,
Down the chimney St. Nicholas
    came with a bound.

He was dressed all in fur
from his head to his foot,

And his clothes were all tarnished
with ashes and soot.

A bundle of toys
   he had flung on his back,

And he looked like a peddler
just opening his pack.

His eyes, how they twinkled!
His dimples, how merry!

His cheeks were like roses,
his nose like a cherry!

His droll little mouth
was drawn up like a bow,

And the beard on his chin
was as white as the snow.

The stump of a pipe
he held tight in his teeth,

And the smoke it encircled
his head like a wreath.

He had a broad face
and a little round belly
That shook when he laughed
like a bowl full of jelly.

He was chubby and plump,
　a right jolly old elf,
And I laughed when I saw him,
　in spite of myself.

A wink of his eye
and a twist of his head
Soon gave me to know
I had nothing to dread.

He spoke not a word
 but went straight to his work
And filled all the stockings,
 then turned with a jerk,

And laying his finger
aside of his nose,
And giving a nod,
up the chimney he rose.

He sprang to his sleigh,
   to his team gave a whistle,
And away they all flew
   like the down of a thistle.

But I heard him exclaim
ere he drove out of sight,

"Happy Christmas to all
and to all a good night!"

The Author and Illustrator

Born July 15, 1779, Clement Clarke Moore was a graduate of Columbia College and a professor of religion. Several of his scholarly works had already appeared in print by 1822, when he wrote a poem about a magical visit from Saint Nicholas as a Christmas gift for his children. Moore likely never meant his poem to have a wider audience than his own family. It was probably a family friend who sent the poem to a local newspaper, the Troy *Sentinel*, where it appeared anonymously with the title "A Visit From Saint Nicholas." It was widely admired and reprinted many times, and finally appeared in 1837, with Clement Moore's name attached, in an anthology that also included several of his other poems.

"The Night Before Christmas," as the poem came to be called, first appeared in book form in 1848, illustrated with austere line drawings by T. C. Boyd. Many other illustrators have interpreted Moore's poem, including Thomas Nash, the political cartoonist who is also responsible for the Republican elephant and the Democratic donkey. His illustrations, done in the 1960s for *Harpers Weekly*, first showed Santa in the familiar outfit we know today: a red suit with white trim and a black belt and boots.

More than a hundred and fifty years after "The Night Before Christmas" was written, Tasha Tudor chose to illustrate the poem in her characteristic period watercolors, with their soft colors and elaborate borders. Her illustrations recreate her own Vermont farmhouse, designed in exact detail after one of 1740. The ornaments on the tree date to the 1840s and were once owned by the artist's grandmother, and readers of her work will already be familiar with her beloved pets, a cat and a corgi, who are present to welcome St. Nicholas as he drops down the chimney.

Filled with charming, whimsical detail—a barn owl who guides St. Nicholas's sleigh to a safe landing, a cat who plays the fiddle so that Santa and a corgi can dance—Tasha Tudor's delightful illustrations are a perfect match for Clement Moore's classic Christmas poem.